The
DUCHESS
and the DRAGON

The
DUCHESS
and the DRAGON

a novel

JAMIE CARIE

B&H
PUBLISHING GROUP
Nashville, Tennessee

ISBN-13: 978-0-7394-9844-6

Published by B&H Publishing Group,
Nashville, Tennessee

Scripture taken from The King James Version.

*This story is dedicated to my sister, Jennifer—who knew
Serena's strength better than I did. To our deep nights sitting
on the deck, dreaming and talking out this story, and to
your power (Him and you together) to remain strong and
faithful and passionate in the face of hardship and opposition.
You are my heroine . . . This one's for you.*

ACKNOWLEDGMENTS

To my editor, Karen Ball—who sweated with me over all the thee's and thou's, the wilts and the arts. I'd like to meet Drake someday too!

To the B&H sales guys and gals—whose home is the road most days, who took these books and ran with them, believing in them. I think of you often; I pray for you often. You are the soldiers on the front lines.

To the bookstore owners and their teams—who are a light and a hope to the communities where they serve. I am humbled to be a part of your ministry.

And to Julie Gwinn, my publicist, a woman who knows the pillar of cloud and the pillar of fire, who moves when He says move and stays when He says stay. You are a multifaceted jewel in His kingdom.

This is a team effort—getting out stories of God's amazing love. I thank God for each of you.

May the side of good win . . .

Chapter One

NORTHUMBERLAND

Drake's fist came down on the massive desk with bone crushing impact. Pain radiated up his arm and into his body, a body trained in the art of bland derision. A body broken now, unable to restrain the fury of this betrayal. He cursed, the sound a quiet hiss in the room. He hung his head, his straight, black hair a curtain over clenched eyes. "May he rot in—"

"Quite right." Charles Blaine, friend and neighbor for as long as Drake could remember, threw himself back into the luxurious cushions of a chair. "Dastardly business, that." He'd said this already. Twice. He repeated it for the third time, staring at the carpet, shaking his head.

Drake swung away from his friend, wishing to be alone, wishing for only the ears of these four walls that he might truly vent his mingled disbelief and outrage. Instead, he took a bracing breath and pulled himself together. He was giving his friends a start.

Control . . . control, man . . . control everything still within grasp. His stomach trembled with the effort.

With a short crack of laughter, he swung back to face his guests, his lip curling, his tone edged in the scorn they all expected. "I should have guessed, I suppose. Stupid of me, really, not to have been prepared. Not to have countered the old man somehow." His voice lowered as he looked down and away from them. "I suppose I never believed he really hated me so much as he let on."

The other two men in the room exchanged glances, obviously at a loss. How could they have any answers for him? The facts spoke for themselves, glaringly real on the scattered pages that lay against the black gloss of the old duke's ornate desk.

Albert Radcliff, the family barrister, mopped at his brow and blew his nose, which was forever running—but had been running with particular need in the strain of the last hour. By some odd twist of fate, Albert was visiting Alnwick Castle when the old duke, Ivor Weston, clutched his chest and collapsed onto the rug, gasping for air like a beached trout.

Drake, too, was home, which was stranger yet. As if all the stars had aligned and arranged the drama so that it might unfold exactly as Ivor wanted. It was fully imaginable that Ivor bargained with the devil for such a favor, some last request in exchange for witnessing a son's destruction.

A favorite pastime of the devil's to be sure.

Charles, though, must have had an angel nudging him. Drake's boyhood friend and neighbor arrived full of excitement about his most recent purchase—a new stallion, a white Lipizzan of famed parentage to add to his stables. They'd been admiring the magnificent animal in the drive when they heard shouts for help from the butler. Drake wasn't sure what he would have done had he not had his friend's bracing support. He shuddered, imagining his hands around the solicitor's throat . . . the new will

Ivor insisted Albert enact thrown into the fire, curling black and smoking, disguised as ash.

No, it didn't bear thinking of.

But Drake couldn't help it, couldn't escape the memory of his father laid out on the floor. The sound of the old man's desperate, rasping command—"New will . . . in the safe!"—rang out in the room like a death knell.

He could only watch, his hand stretched out toward his father, while waves of shock rippled through his body. But Ivor was intent on only one thing. He lifted his head off the floor and grasped his solicitor's hand in a vein-popping, eye-bulging frenzy. "It is what I want . . . nothing else will do. Find it, Albert."

Drake moved into his father's field of vision and knelt down beside him, reaching for his hand.

Ivor jerked away, placing the hand on his rasping chest, then finally turned toward Drake. Ivor stared at him—really looked into his eyes as he'd never done before. Drake recoiled as his father's mask of indifference was stripped away by death's honesty, exposing the truth of feverish eyes and compressed lips, revealing a long-awaited, gleeful vengeance.

The old duke even cackled in his excitement, a grating, harsh sound that was cut off with a gasp for air. He'd started to speak, then gave up and died—that leering smile lingering around his now frozen lips.

So sinister was the scene that both Drake and Albert backed away from the body as though it were black and stinking with the plague. They'd looked at one another for several shocked moments, then made for the safe.

And now they knew.

Each person in the room knew the depths of his father's hatred for him. By the end of the month the whole of society would learn the shocking news that Drake Alexander Weston, the only child of the Duke of Northumberland, had mysteriously, inexplicably, been cut from the will.

Albert stood, his hands shaking as he restacked the papers. He looked up at Drake, strain deepening the creases around his mouth and eyes, his age-mottled hand lying flat on the restacked documents.

"A nasty piece of business if ever I saw one. It is not the will he had me draw up years ago, my . . . lord." He choked on the title, throat working up and down under the loose skin of his neck, then coughed into a hastily pulled handkerchief. That he should now be calling Drake "your grace" instead of "my lord" was one of many mockeries yet in store for Drake.

Drake waved him off. "Never mind, Albert. I suppose I will have to get used it. I suppose I should be happy to have a title a'tall." He said the words in a clear tone, but had to turn away from their staring faces, his stomach rolling. He fought the nausea threatening his throat.

Unsure of his way, he found himself walking to one of the many masterpieces displayed on a far wall. Van Dyck's lush *Samson and Delilah* hung suspended like a scene come to life against the swirling mother-of-pearl panels of the walls. He stared at the raw beauty of the scene. Here was a man with strength, the kind of strength to bring down kingdoms. But Samson had his weakness, and Drake? Now he knew his. Tears welled up behind his eyes. He'd only wanted to please his father, to know that he was proud of the man Drake had become. But it wasn't to be. Now, all he could see was a painting that would never belong to him. A father's love that he would never have. Why? His mind struggled to grasp it. Why all the grooming and pretending? The years at Eton and then Cambridge, the best schools in England, the military career in His Majesty's Royal Navy, the constant displeasure at any show of emotion other than self-satisfaction for some material gain. All the torment he'd gone through that made him into the man he now was. He'd thought it was to make him into a duke. He'd thought it was to mold him into a man like his father.

He'd thought wrong.

Drake paced across the rich Savonnerie rug, woven for this very room and placed to complement the gleaming mosaic flooring. His father spent much of his life in this room, overseeing its most minute detail—all part of the grand scheme to reflect the power and honor of the Seat of Northumberland. Drake's gaze swept the room, trying to grasp some hidden meaning.

He remembered, as a boy, when he'd really seen it for the first time. The richness of color and texture could be overwhelming to someone unused to such luxury. He'd seen the awe on their guests' faces many times, and he'd always taken pride in the fact that someday . . . someday it would be him greeting that awed visitor; it would be his room that brought gasps of wonder from men and women who could but dream of such wealth.

A trickle of sweat ran down his back as he realized he was gasping for air. This place . . . it was breathtaking. Was there any place on earth more perfect? Alnwick Castle. It was his promised inheritance.

His.

Inheritance.

He lurched back toward the men, trying to wear the familiar devil-may-care attitude but feeling like a carefully constructed house of cards whose bottom strut had been jerked away.

His eyes were drawn to the desk where the destruction of his life lay. The new will, confident in its strong, slashing handwriting, glared at him. The desk, a work of art, made of ebony wood covered with tortoise shell and inlaid with gilded brass, mocked him. A jade sculpture of a Chinese dragon stood on one corner, ornate and ferocious in design. It used to frighten him as a child.

Now he knew there were far more terrifying things in life than dragons.

A marble quill and ink set stood now silent near the top center edge.

Weapons used to destroy his future.

A clear glass sphere sat on the other corner along with several dogs, some intricate blown glass, some porcelain, others pewter and silver—all made in the image of his father's only passion outside power and wealth: his dogs.

His father's favorite, Hunter, had received the attention and praise Drake had longed for as a child. He had been secretly glad when the dog died, but it hadn't mattered. There was little Drake could do to earn a word of praise from the stoic Ivor Weston, fourth Duke of Northumberland.

Now Drake realized it was far worse than he had suspected. His father hadn't just disliked him. He'd harbored a deep hatred for his son. The question remained: Why?

Drake stared at the pages willing them to reveal some clue. His father's handwriting, so stark and clear, proved he had been keen until his last breath. The hope that he had gone mad held no relief. Nothing could explain what he had done—expect pure maliciousness. Drake, his hands now braced on each polished edge, stared at the desk, in the room his father loved, and felt his barely constrained hurt and rage break through the barrier of his will. With a violent roar, he swept the pages and decorative accoutrements onto the floor. Glass and porcelain shattered; papers fluttered through the air like the feathers of a bird caught mid-flight by a bullet.

He swung around to face his startled friends. He'd let the caged animal out, but he no longer cared. Let them pity him. "There must be a way out of this! I refuse to let him do this to me!" Looking at the barrister he commanded, "Burn the will. We will use the other. The one you wrote up years ago. No one will know."

Albert only shook his head and looked down. "Nasty business, that. Can't do it."

Charles leapt up, clearing his throat, then made for the crystal decanter to pour a stout drink. Avoiding the broken glass, he picked his way back to Drake's side. "Easy, man," he said in a voice meant to soothe, "drink this."

Drake shook his head as if clearing it from a fog, took hold of the drink, and gulped it in one swallow. Hot talons of fire burned his throat, but he was glad. Glad of any sensation other than the dark pit of despair that awaited him. Setting the glass down on the now barren desk, he walked to a chair and sat. He closed his eyes and then dropped his head into his hands, no longer trying to make sense of it all, only knowing searing pain.

Charles cleared his throat. "Look here, Albert, is there nothing we can do? No way around the will?"

Drake looked up, saw Albert's gaze dart around the room as if it could help him. Shaking his head he said finally, "I am afraid not, the will is very clear, supersedes the other. The ducal estate and title is to be given to the, um, the cousin, Lord Randolph." His voice lowered as he corrected himself. "His grace, Randolph Weston." He mopped at his damp brow with his ever ready handkerchief as his eyes wandered over to the crystal decanter as if he, too, needed a drink.

Drake stood abruptly, "Do not call him by that title within my hearing, do you understand? Never again."

7

Albert nodded and continued. "Sorry, but you must accustom yourself to hearing it. It will soon be common knowledge." Albert shook his gray head and looked at the floor. "If only you had a brother, then we could at least keep it in the immediate family."

Drake's head shot up. "What was that?"

Albert reddened, a vein pulsing blue in his forehead. "I am sorry, my lord. Pointless to think, much less speak of such things."

"What is this about a brother?"

"Only that if you had a legitimate brother, my lord, your cousin would then become heir presumptive and the title and estate might go to the sibling as the next of kin after you."

"Your father hasn't a pregnant mistress hidden around the place, has he?" Charles drawled from his chair.

Drake rose and began pacing the length of the carpet. Giving Charles a scowl, he directed his question to Albert. "How so, when my father dictated in his will that everything be given to my cousin?"

"The king would doubtless override the will if a more direct heir were discovered. A few carefully placed words and documents, birth records and such, and I believe King George would look the other way and allow the sibling to inherit." Albert shrugged. "Alas, there is no other heir."

Drake stopped pacing in front of Albert and looked into the old man's face with a slow smile. "Perhaps there will be." He spoke more to himself than the others. "Yes, a dear, little brother."

Rubbing his chin thoughtfully, he felt his smile grow. Of course. It was perfect. The best part of this plan was that his father, for all his wealth and determination, would not have the last laugh after all.

That distinct pleasure would belong to Drake.

Chapter Two

The men stared at Drake Alexander Weston, Earl of Warwick, wide-eyed. He had cracked, the disappointment too much.

Drake knew that's what they were thinking and gave them the same smile he'd worn since he was ten, the world-weary smile of omniscient confidence. "Who knows of my father's death?"

The two men exchanged glances. The duke's body lay in the next room. The physician had been sent for, but little else was done as they had been so intent to carry out those last words.

Charles spoke up first. "Aside from the three of us?" He shrugged. "A couple of household servants and soon Doctor Canton. The man has only been dead a little above an hour. I thought we would notify the parson first thing in the morning."

Drake raised his hand. "No. No one is to know anything yet."

Charles stared hard at his friend. "What the devil are you thinking of, Drake?"

"We will keep the old man's death a secret—" he couldn't restrain a smile; this was too perfect—"until I can marry."

"Marry?" Albert frowned at him. "What good will that do?"

"No good at all if I marry as myself."

His friends' expressions told him they feared for his sanity.

"However, a great deal of good—" he drew out the suspense—"should I marry as my father. Even more good when I produce a child. Namely, my brother."

Albert choked on his water. Charles stared at Drake in wide-eyed disbelief. "You can't be serious. It will never wash. First off, how do you propose to keep the old man's death a secret?"

"As it has been stated many times before," Drake said sardonically, "I am, in appearance at least, the very image of my father. With a little theatrical makeup and some padding—" he shrugged, looking down at his wide chest and flat stomach— "I will look enough like him to make an occasional appearance. From a distance, of course. I am quite certain I can even fool the servants."

Charles shook his head, "And what of the servants who know? You'll never be able to keep news of this import quiet. You're talking out of desperation, man!"

"The desperate are often the most cunning." Drake wasn't in the least deterred. "Listen to me. My servants are completely loyal to me. I am certain I can depend upon their cooperation. The doctor, however, will have already been told and will have to be bought."

"But how . . . ?"

Drake ignored Charles's sputtering confusion. "I will marry immediately, as my father, and upon finding the most fertile noblewoman in all of England, I will, God willing, bring a son, a dear baby brother, into this world. A short time later, my father will die from a withering disease that has kept him ill and in bed for months. The end result will be that my brother will inherit the dukedom. I will, of course manage the estate for him until he comes of age, at which time I will turn it over to him." After finishing his case Drake looked at his friends, satisfaction filling him, replacing the despair. He almost chuckled aloud, knowing this was the final and most perfect irony of all.

"I will give up what is rightfully mine to one person and one person only. My own son."

THE DAWN, THREE days later, found Drake on the third story balcony of Alnwick Castle, having a hearty breakfast of ham, eggs, buttered toast, potatoes thick with cream, and coffee. Whenever he was home and the weather permitted, he took his morning meal outdoors: on a balcony, terrace, or one of the many garden spots. He preferred these places over the stuffy red-and-gold dining room he shared with his father on rare occasions.

This morning he was engrossed in his newspaper, calm as any other morning. And why not? Having convinced Charles and Albert of his scheme he had little doubt he could convince others. And convince them he had. He smiled in memory, the words of the newspaper in front of him growing dim. Soon after their conversation had ended, Drake called the servants who knew of Ivor's death to the study. They were given a condensed version of the plan and asked for loyalty, even as a weighty purse of leather was pressed into each hand. The doctor had been a bit harder to convince, but Drake was certain he could depend on him now that he had silenced the man's conscience with an even heavier purse. The good doctor would never have to treat another case of consumption or deliver another baby as long as he lived if he didn't want to.

The next step in this lunacy was to locate some padding, cosmetics, and the wherewithal to use them. The unaware servants were told his father had gone to London for a few weeks. Drake calculated that would give him time to prepare and practice for the appearances he would make as his father. But the greatest challenge would be to find the perfect woman who would pose as his father's wife. Ivor should fall in love while in London, he mused, and come back remarried. The question was . . . to whom?

Drake allowed his mind to travel over the faces of the women in his life—beautiful women of varied backgrounds and temperaments, but having in common the grasping, avaricious character that dominated the ladies of his set. There had been many over the years, but many more opportunities for romantic liaisons that he had flatly refused. He was as calculated in his dalliance as he was in every other aspect of his life. He could have—perhaps even *should* have—chosen one of them to become his bride by now. But he'd enjoyed the life he led too much to consider that it could change so completely.

Still, now that he had to choose one and quickly, he found himself unable to do so. Lana, his current mistress, was an earl's daughter. She would be delighted—no, ecstatic. But he didn't think he wanted to trust such a secret with her. She was too demanding, too moody, and much too talkative. He needed a quiet woman—submissive and sweet. Someone who would accept this scheme and him as a temporary husband without questioning him to death over it. Once the child was born, Ivor could be put to rest in truth, and Drake would end his relationship with the woman. He would live in London, visiting occasionally to watch over the upbringing of his son.

Or rather . . . his brother.

He chuckled. It *was* preposterous, when he thought of all the implications. But the woman would remain a duchess, living here in the splendor that was Alnwick Castle. He was confident he could find any number of females willing to accept the terms of such a bizarre proposal.

Rubbing his freshly shaved chin, he leaned back in his wrought-iron chair and contemplated his other feminine acquaintances. He really should marry a virgin. Had to be certain it was his child that inherited the dukedom. And, much to his surprise, he realized he wanted someone who would be faithful, at least for the duration of the scheme. An innocent who would bear him a child and then become a rich dowager duchess, raising her child in the quiet countryside of Northumberland.

It was more than many women of the ton had.

An infinitesimal movement from Drake's hand brought his footman to his side. Drake gestured for a refill of coffee and indicated his need of more eggs. They appeared, at the perfect temperature, in the exact amount he would have wanted on his plate and in his fine imported Indonesian cup. Drake picked up his fork, eyes on his food, and nodded his dismissal.

Sipping from his cup, he sank back into contemplating candidates for a wife when a slight rapping sound at the outside of the door to his balcony caused him to turn, a frown tugging at his brows.

"Yes?" he barked at the shadow behind the wavy glass.

A reed-like man slipped through the opening. His shoes were dirt encrusted, his clothes filthy, a grimy hat turned round and round in his hands. Drake resisted the urge to curl his lip. "What is it, man? Can't you see I'm at my breakfast?" This was hardly the sign of a well-run establishment. How had the man gotten beyond his stalwart butler? "Where is Crudnell?"

"Pardon, milord, I begged an audience with ye. I heard tell of . . . well . . . I know ye 'ad some trouble . . . t'other night." His voice dropped to a whisper, while he glanced over his shoulder. His gaze took on a greedy glint as he met Drake's eyes for the first time. "I was 'oping to get in on the blunt. In exchange for my keepin' quiet about the plot to get your fine self an heir, if you take my meanin', milord."

Drake went hot, then cold. He stared at the man. The audacity! To be called on the carpet by someone of this person's ilk. Drake turned in his chair, facing the little man.

This, too, was his father's fault. Rage returned, rushing to his cheeks and throbbing in his head. That he should be cornered by the likes of this fellow, in his own house, on his own balcony—

It was too much! Surging from his chair like a dragon awakening from the comforts of his lair, Drake stalked over to tower above the man. "You, you sodden stench of humanity, will not utter a word about anything to anyone or you will never be able to utter a word again! Do *you* take *my* meaning?"

The man backed up, cowering, but to Drake's astonishment he rallied. "I'll not leave without the same blunt the doctor got from ye. And I know how much it was."

The doctor. He should have known the old fool would be the weak link in this mess. "The doctor told you?"

"Not exactly, milord, but I overheard 'im telling 'is wife. I work for 'em. They was talkin' with the windows open, milord."

Black dots of rage filled Drake's vision. He advanced—breathing hard through his nostrils. If this little man knew, soon the whole countryside would as well. His plans to reach his own bit of heaven crumbled like the tower of Babel. "You are very sure of yourself." Drake's words held quiet menace. "Whom have you told?"

The man shrugged nervously, "Only my wife, milord—just to safeguard my protection whilst I was 'ere."

"And whom, pray tell, has your wife told?"

"N–n–no one." Then, seeing Drake advance, he amended, "I can't rightly say, she being a woman and all."

Drake roared and took another step, backing the man up to the railing. "So you think you are safe from me?"

The man glanced over his shoulder at the stone terrace below. Terror filled his eyes.

Drake felt his own power. It would be so easy . . .

He took another step, closing the gap of reason that held his hands back, and leaned over the man. The scoundrel bowed back, his waist pressed against the railing, his feet on tiptoe.

The sun felt hot on the back of Drake's neck and he watched, transfixed as a trickle of sweat beaded on the little man's brow, rolling slowly down his dirty face. Time seemed to hold its breath as Drake wavered, feeling the hardness of the tiles under his feet, seeing a spot of peeling black paint on the railing beneath his hand. A sudden breeze rose up, making his hair dance around his face. Suspended, Drake stared into the man's eyes—and felt with astonishing clarity the reality of holding another's life in his hands.

Take it—just as your father took yours.

The man's face wavered, became Ivor's, full of scorn and laughing from the grave. Drake's insides shifted, then shattered. It was gone. Everything . . . gone.

With a sudden move, Drake reared back, away from the man.

A sudden shriek split the air—an awful sound that startled Drake out of his trance. One glance told Drake the terrible truth: The man couldn't recover his balance quickly enough. Before Drake could move, the little man, eyes wide with fright, stretched out an arm toward Drake—and was gone. Toppled over the rail. Another scream, and then a dull thud.

The sound echoed across the stone terrace below and carried into the lush green gardens.

Drake looked at the fingers of his right hand, grasping into thin air. Stunned, he peered over the rail at the inert body, one leg lying cocked in a position that spoke of severe injury. A sick nausea rose from his belly to his throat. He pressed his fist to his mouth. Why hadn't he been able to grasp the man's arm? He had only meant to frighten him . . . hadn't he?

Before he had the chance to answer the questions, the echo of hurried footsteps sounded behind him.

"My lord, we heard a scream . . ."

His footman and butler stood at rigid attention at his back. Drake turned slowly to face them. "He fell. My visitor slipped over the railing and fell." The words rang as false as they were. The careful, blank stares from his servants assured him they did not believe him.

Crudnell stammered, which only added to the strange reality that was now his life. "W—w—what shall we d—d—do, my lord? Fetch the doctor?"

Fear and panic rushed in.

How strange, this feeling of fear. Drake couldn't remember feeling it since he was a small boy. It was . . . immobilizing. He couldn't think how to answer his butler. Plowing through the servants, he ignored their presence and fled to his bedchamber.

Closing the door behind him he leaned against it, panting as if he'd just run the breadth of his property.

Think, man!

There was no question that he was responsible for the man's death. When the entire tale came out—and it would, of that he had no doubt—they would hang him or worse, send him to a hellish life in Newgate Prison.

He tore himself away from the door and rushed to the dressing chamber to search for a trunk. He threw clothes and stockings and neck cloths out of his way, utterly panicked. He had never packed for himself in his life and felt impotent rage at the knowledge that he might require help finding something in which to pack his things.

No, he couldn't let the servants see him like this.

A small trunk stood in the far corner of the dressing room; he dragged it out. Opening it, he inhaled sharply. It was his childhood trunk. Something he hadn't seen for years and hadn't even known still existed. There lay the boyhood treasures he'd cherished and long since forgotten. With no time to waste, he pawed through it. Most went to the floor in a pile: a wooden yo-yo he'd gotten at a fair, a few books, a battered sailboat and some half-finished sketches. Near the bottom lay a miniature portrait of his mother.

This and a lace handkerchief embroidered with ivy and her initials, LW, intertwined in the leaves, he left in the corner of the trunk. Turning to the mass of clothing, Drake chose some practical and some formal clothes. He didn't know where he was going or if he would ever return.

A sudden pounding on the door startled him.

"Leave me!"

Footsteps padded away down the hall. Drake redoubled his efforts, cramming his signet ring onto his finger and a heavy leather pouch of coins in his pocket. He would get more money from his solicitor in London, when he could. This would tide him over until he knew the lay of the land.

Shouted voices drew his attention to the window. A carriage had just stopped in front of the castle and a tall, stately gentleman was descending. Drake peered out, half hidden by the heavy, royal blue window coverings. Justin Abbot? A dark curse escaped his lips. What was the king's lackey, a powerful member of the Cabinet Council and a person Drake only acquainted himself with when necessity demanded it, doing here now? Drake had heard that the man was in the north on King George's business, but he hadn't expected to see him at Alnwick.

For him to appear now meant certain disaster.

It had only been three days since his father's death, but it was possible Abbot had heard something and was coming to investigate. Add the incriminating evidence of a dead man on his terrace and . . .

Drake jerked away from the window, seeing that his hands were clenched so tight his nails were imbedded into his palms. He must not panic. And yet, it seemed the very earth was opening beneath his feet.

He rushed to the packed trunk and shut its lid with a bang. Oh, for more time to plan and think! There were papers in the library he would like to have, more money, valuables he could sell later if need be. But no time. He locked the trunk, his fingers fumbling in haste and frustration.

Drake hoisted the trunk. Was it possible? Was he now carrying his only belongings in the world? The hall outside his room was quiet and deserted, but he could hear voices drifting up from the stairway. Quickly, he slunk toward the backstairs. Maude, an upstairs maid, was coming up. She took a breath to speak at the sight of him, stopping suddenly when Drake shook his head and put a finger to his mouth. "You did not see me, is that clear, Maude?"

She bobbed her pretty head, eyes wide, and whispered back. "There's a man here to see you, my lord. From the king. How could he have known so quickly?"

"Let's not jump to conclusions, Maude. What's to know? Listen, reason would have it that I put some time and distance between this situation and myself. You understand?"

Maude nodded again, though her brow puckered.

"Good, now let us go down together and find a horse. I may be in need of your assistance."

Even as the two hurried down to a back entrance leading to the kitchens, Drake could hear a commotion coming from the front of the house.

"Now," Drake commanded, "as quick as you can and without being noticed, run ahead and tell Henry to saddle Talisman for me. Then lead him toward the south garden gate. If you are seen and anyone remarks upon it, let him loose and I will find him. Understand?"

Maude nodded again, "Yes, my lord."

"Very well, now go."

Drake watched as she hurried to the stable. Once out of sight, he held to the shadows of the house, making his way into the garden, careful to stay beneath the foliage of bushes and trees. At one point he thought he heard a shout coming from the house, but he wasn't certain. Pulse accelerating, he hid behind a dense wall of hedges, peering over the top and waiting for movement from the direction of the stable.

Part of him wondered if he shouldn't go back and brazen it out. Running only made him look guilty. And yet, the thought of the cold wall of Newgate pressed against his back made him happy to see Maude rounding the corner of the stable. She led his prized thoroughbred, an animal as fast as he was enduring, and Drake silently thanked whatever fate watched out for him.

He held his breath as the pair hurried through open ground. When they reached him, he gave her a quick peck on the cheek and said, "Not a word to anyone, Maude. You have done me good service this day. I will not forget you."

She blushed and nodded, starry eyed. "But when will you return? What will happen to all of us, my lord?"

Drake grimaced. What, indeed? "I do not know, Maude. I wish I could tell you, but I just don't know."

After strapping down the trunk Drake swung up to the familiar creak of his saddle. Talisman galloped several yards, then Drake turned and took one last look at the manicured lawns, the formal gardens, the imposing castle that stretched into the blue of the sky.

An inheritance lost.

Drake turned from it all, his heart leaden, not knowing if he would ever see it again, and put the spur to his horse.

He did not look back.

Chapter Three

LONDON

rake huddled against the brick building of his solicitor's office, the sharp edges of the wall digging into his back. The hardness reminded him of the stone terrace the man had fallen to. It never left him for long, this feeling of guilt. Sometimes it was a weighty pressure against his chest that made him struggle for a deep breath. Other times, a deep sorrow, a grief so profound that he couldn't think how to go on with the ordinary business of where to eat, or whether he should stay at Charles's house, or what to do next. It was as if he'd plummeted from another world . . . into a hellish world.

Rain-soaked and cold, he clenched his teeth until his jaws ached. A high-sprung carriage with a coat of arms emblazoned on the side passed, splashing water onto his boots, adding to his sodden, heavy feel. A woman's laughter drifted from inside the carriage—that kind of laughter that was pleased with itself, confident in its invulnerability.

He used to laugh like that.

A sudden feeling, a flash of insight struck him of how it might feel to live on these cold, unfriendly streets. Truly, he could stay here all night, huddled on this corner, and no one would care.

He looked at the scene around him with new sight. Across the way a couple stood, the woman beautiful and smiling up into the handsome face of her companion. She beckoned a serving girl to come closer with the umbrella. Her bracelet entangled on the handle as the slight servant maneuvered the umbrella as close as she dared. The woman jerked her hand back, her face not quite so lovely now as she berated the servant with harsh words. Drake watched as the servant's face turned ashen and panicked. Had he done that countless times without noticing?

The theatre must have just let out, Drake thought bitterly. Servants held carriage doors open, waiting with warm blankets to ensure their betters were comfortable. All the trappings of what used to be his life.

He resisted the urge to slam his fist into the wall. If he could just get up to Albert's business quarters, he could at least gain the comforts of a fire.

It had been two weeks since his hasty flight from Northumberland. After reaching London, Drake took up residence with Charles for a few days. He'd hated to come to London, knowing his chances for capture increased with every mile he came within the king's court, but it was the best—no, the *only*—place to liquefy his assets and hear news that would either bring him out into the open or exile him from the continent.

The latter had soon proved true.

It hadn't been long before Justin Abbot returned, questioning his closest friends, saying only that he was looking for Drake. The noose drew ever tighter, and Drake knew he had to get out of London. England too. But to travel any distance, he needed more money than he had been able to spirit away. And to gain the comforts of a heavier purse, he needed to see Albert.

He had waited all day for the cover of darkness and now stood there, skulking in the shadows like a common thief, waiting for this theatre crowd to disperse.

Finally, he slipped around the corner of the building and hurried to the entrance, rain dripping from the lowered brim of his hat. He ducked into the hall and drew a deep breath. The marble floor and tall ceiling caused his footsteps to echo through the deserted place. Head down, he followed the familiar path to Albert's office.

"Drake," came a scratchy voice from an inner room, "is that you, then? In here."

"Albert?" He didn't sound well. Drake picked up a lantern, which cast a gloomy glow in the outer office, and crept toward the inner sanctum.

At the sight of a single candle lighting Albert's craggy face, Drake released a held breath. His friend was alone.

"Put the light out," Albert wheezed. "Abbot was sniffing around earlier today." Pulling a handkerchief from his pocket, he dabbed at his dripping nose.

Drake studied the corners of the room before obeying. Then, setting the lantern on the floor, he took the seat across from Albert. "Are you being followed? Watched?"

"No . . . no, I was not here when Abbot came by today, but he will be back." Albert pushed a bottle across the desk. "You look frozen through. Here, have some Madeira."

Drake wished it were something stronger but grasped the bottle. He hadn't allowed himself to spend any unnecessary money and the restraint had been surprisingly difficult. He had always prided himself of the mastery of his will, but recently discovered the magnetic pull of the forbidden. The liquor slid down his throat with smooth familiarity, bringing a rosy warmth to his chest. "Do you have the money?"

Albert sighed. "'Tis not as much as you hoped, my lord. But I didn't want to cause questions by overtly rippling your financial waters. There seem to be eyes and ears everywhere." He slid a heavy purse across the desk.

Drake felt the weight in his hand and glanced inside. "This will not last a year."

Albert nervously rubbed the loose skin of his jaw line. "I shall send you more as I can. I have not been able to learn what they know, but I know they have not given up looking for you." He leaned across the table toward Drake. "We must get you out of England, my boy."

Leave England? Had his life really come to that? Drake dropped his head in his hands and drew in a deep, ragged breath. "What of the shares in the East India Company. Have you sold them?" When Albert didn't answer Drake looked up, eyes narrowed at the old retainer. "Have you managed anything else for me?"

Albert cleared his throat, his gaze darting away from Drake's scrutiny. "I have a plan to buy you some time until this debacle is sorted through. You're not going to like it, but it will get you out of the country with no one the wiser."

Drake found he had no voice, could only stare.

"There is a ship, *The Prince Royal*, leaving for America in two days. If the king's men are watching the roads and ships leaving England, you would do well to adopt a disguise of some sort. They will be looking for an aristocrat with the usual trappings of nobility. The captain of this ship is signing on indentured servants." He hesitated at Drake's dark look, cleared his throat and continued. "I know it sounds intolerable, but it may work. They will not be looking for you among the masses of poor going over to be indentured. Once safely in America, I can send you more money and, while you are away, I will see what I can do about getting your name cleared. When we know what the king is thinking, we can act accordingly."

Drake stood and paced the small room. "If you think a pardon is possible, I should stay and face the charges."

Albert's jowls swayed as he shook his head. "Drake . . . I do not think that would be wise. We need time for the facts to come out and for tempers to subside. You *must* leave the country."

Drake placed his hands on either side of the desk and leaned toward Albert. "How could this have happened? Albert, *tell* me. Am I not my father's son? Have you but to look at me to see his face? I see him every time I look in the mirror. Why did he do this to me?"

Albert looked down at his clasped hands in his lap, his lips pressed together in a thin line. "I do not know, my lord. I do not know." He paused, sudden speculation in his gaze as he looked back up at Drake. "You have just reminded me of an old rumor. I have never put any stock in it, mind you, but . . ."

"Tell me."

Albert shrugged. "Rumors are rarely reliable, Drake."

"You will tell me regardless."

"Well, your father did have two brothers, did he not?"

"Yes, Cousin Randolph's father, Clinton, dead for many years now, and Richard, the youngest brother who lives in Bristol, I believe. Quiet man, I've met him only once. What of it?"

"The tale was that your mother fell in love with Richard. She was already betrothed to your father, had been since she was a young girl, but hardly knew him. Not long after the marriage

Richard came to see them, and your father was away. I do not know the details and I certainly cannot believe it true—"

A deep dread made Drake's stomach tremble.

"—but some say you were conceived during his visit."

No! The denial echoed inside him. Impossible. He couldn't be anything other than Ivor's son. It was unimaginable. "How could anyone think such a thing? There must be more to the story." That anyone should question his parentage on the simple fact that his mother was alone with his uncle for a time was absurd.

"The only fact that gives the tale some credence is that when your father returned, he banished Richard from Northumberland and said he would never see him again. No one knew exactly why, but rumor was rife, as it always is in such cases."

"Preposterous!" But the quaking inside him grew, threatened to become a full-blown panic. He thought of his mother, a sad, pale wraith of a woman, possessing an ethereal beauty that seemed to fade each year until she was a ghost on her deathbed. And always, that faraway look in her eyes . . .

His hand, a balled fist in his lap, shook so that he had to press his other hand against it. He looked down, willing a stillness into his body. He would not, could not think of his mother doing such a thing. She would have never betrayed his father in such a manner. She would never have made her son illegitimate—*would* she?

Drake stood and paced, pulling his shattered emotions into brisk action. "So your plan is to indenture me to the colonies? I, Drake Alexander Weston, reared to a dukedom, shall become a servant?" He let his mockery show in his smile as he looked down at the older man from his full height of six foot three inches.

"My lord . . . that is, I see little alternative."

"No!" Drake turned to the desk, snatched up the half-empty bottle of Madeira and flung it against the wall.

Albert sat in stunned silence, fear lighting his eyes. Drake struggled to control his emotions. He caught a glimpse of himself in a small mirror hanging on the opposite wall. Wild-eyed, unshaven, and so angry. The man who stared back was not a man he knew. The careful control bred into him since birth was gone. In its place he saw a fire-breathing dragon capable of murder.

Yes—he saw a murderer, and it terrified him.

Breathing fast he flung himself into the chair, his hands balling into fists. "What shall I do? What would you have me do?"

Albert rose from his chair and handed Drake a piece of paper, then laid a bracing hand on Drake's shoulder. "Sign this, son. Buy some time. It is your best hope."

Drake stared at the paper. Had the world gone mad? Sign the paper. Indeed.

Fingers shaking, he took the quill from Albert's hand and dipped it in the black ink. Just as he pressed tip to paper, Albert halted him. "Sign your name as Drake Winslow. You dare not go by Drake Weston any longer."

He stared at the tip of the quill, the ink so black and ready to drip, wondering if he could do it. Then he hunched over the page and scrawled the foreign name.

"It is over," he whispered into the dark.

DRAKE STOOD WITH the rest of the indentured in a long line on the docks of the River Thames. The mid-morning shadows of the warehouses fell across them, shading the sun as it rose beyond the Tower of London. London Bridge sat in the distant west, a familiar black outline against the gray sky. How many times had he clattered over that stone edifice and thought nothing of its magnitude, its memories of such a great city. Now he might never see it again.

Turning toward the west and his new future, Drake felt a shaft of doubt for his own sanity. Two ships bobbed in front of them on the dark green waters of the Thames. One, massive and sturdy, was being loaded with supplies, her hull sitting low in the water. Next to it floated their ship. Studying that rickety craft with the eyes of a man who had financed and inspected many a cargo vessel, Drake fought the urge to slink out of line and back into the shadows.

Being indentured was the least of his worries. His shaky resolve to follow Albert's plan threatened to dissolve into the wisps of a nightmare. Mere weeks ago he wouldn't have considered trusting a barrel of tea aboard this heap and now he was boarding it himself? Ludicrous! And yet, what choice did he really have?

He looked around at his companions, dock workers and passersby, half hoping for some miracle to jump out and save him. Instead, his feet shuffled forward with the rest.

A sudden shout drew his attention and that of his companions. A constable was leading a man, hands tied behind his back, down a gangplank and back to shore. The constable jerked to a halt, his eyes sharp as he scanned the crowd. Drake ducked his head. The hat he wore was pulled down low over his eyes, two weeks' worth of beard darkened his cheeks and chin, but he was tall and stood out. His chances of being caught in such a disguise were slim, but still, sharp tension stiffened his spine. The colonies were better than Newgate.

Or so he kept telling himself.

A woman behind him coughed, a rasping sound that boded ill. His skin crawled of its own accord as he took an involuntary step forward. They were a downtrodden lot, his fellow passengers. The stench of poverty hung like a bleak aura around them. Drake shuffled even further forward, hunching down, allowing the hollow feeling in his gut to reach his eyes.

No one he knew could possibly recognize him. He scarcely recognized himself.

His mind fixated on the murder—those few moments replaying in his head with razor-sharp clarity. Sixteen long days since an interrupted breakfast and a poor man's death. Days filled with watching and waiting, but Drake knew not what he was waiting for. Sixteen days of anxiety gnawing at him till he'd lost so much weight that his clothes hung from his frame in heavy folds. Sixteen nights of fitful sleep for fear the nightmares would come. Nightmares that strove to ensnare him and pull him down into madness where murderers belonged. Truth be told, he had little need for a disguise; his mask of wretchedness was only too real.

They drew closer to the gangplank—a wet, narrow board slippery from muddy feet. The dank, fishy smell common to the Thames assaulted his nostrils; the screech of seagulls above their heads grated in his ears. A mother and two small children set foot upon the gangplank, and Drake found himself holding his breath. The youngest child, a little girl, began to cry and wouldn't move; the boy clung to his mother's skirts threatening to topple them all.

"Get a move on!" A shrill voice from behind yelled.

The woman took another step, but the younger of her children swayed. All eyes in line watched as the mother screamed and grasped a fistful of the girl's shirt. There was a collective sigh of relief as they righted themselves.

Before Drake could think better of it, he stepped out of line and was walking to the front.

"'Ey! What's to do, 'ere?"

"You cain't step ahead in line!"

Drake stilled the complainers with a look, the mantle of authority still draping him.

One woman nudged the man beside her. "Who's he think he is, eh?"

Drake leapt onto the gangplank, swinging the tiny girl into the crook of one arm. The lad looked up at him with big, round eyes as Drake grasped his hand. "Step lively now, my boy. You can do it."

The child nodded, chubby cheeks rounding in a smile. When they reached the other side, Drake jumped down onto the deck of the ship. The girl in his arm hadn't moved during the crossing, but now cried out for her mother. Drake turned to the woman and helped guide her down to the deck. He then deposited the toddler into her arms. "Your children, madam."

The woman stood, mouth open for a moment, and then blushed. "Oh thank ye, kind sir. I was so afeared they'd be drowned afore we ever begun."

Drake inclined his head, then turned from her—and stilled. Countless numbers of eyes were upon him. *Fool! How could you have forgotten? Can you not for a moment remember who you are now, what you are supposed to be?* This was going to be impossible! He gritted his teeth and turned away, following the others down into the hold to claim a bunk.

A rickety ladder, a creaking, swaying floor, a dark hold, a place where the air didn't move. This would be his new home.

It took a few moments for his eyes to adjust. He stared, heart sinking, at row upon row of double or triple-tiered bunks. Alnwick

Castle, its grandeur, its imperial force against nature and man, rose up to taunt him. Against all will, a sob grew in his throat . . . followed immediately by shame. Making a quick judgment, Drake staked his claim on an outside row with easy access to the ladder leading up on deck. Some of the others claimed a bed and then returned to the deck for a last look at England before sailing. Drake thought better of leaving his belongings unattended, so he sat on the bed and waited. It wouldn't do to court more trouble by standing up on deck for all to see him—a fugitive, a dependent on the winds of fate, a poor wretch leaving his homeland.

His new home amounted to about six feet long and two feet wide, his bed a thin straw-filled pallet on a rickety looking frame. Underneath the frame was the only space to store his belongings and the meager supplies he had purchased for the journey that would take about fourteen weeks. They were packed in here like slaves, except slaves were shackled. Drake's appreciation for freedom suddenly made itself known, startling him.

Embarrassment stole up his neck as he realized that he wanted to collapse—to lie on this shoddy iron bed and wallow in self-pity like he hadn't since he wore gowns. Instead, he took a shaky breath and steeled himself. He would make it to America, get out of this ridiculous indentured servant business altogether, and begin a new life. What he would do to support himself once the meager funds in his trunk ran out he didn't know. Still . . . news traveled slowly. Perhaps he could join the other impoverished nobility on the new continent.

He wrapped the thin blanket about him, lay back, and closed his eyes, hoping sleep—and the nightmares—wouldn't come just yet.

Chapter Four

Serena stared out her bedroom window, taking in the late fall scene of her yard and street. The leaves were mostly fallen now, lying in brown, tumbled heaps, blown about by the breeze. An old, gnarled tree filled the north corner of the yard, where a wooden swing twirled, the wind its only occupant. She had swung on that swing countless times, reaching her toes up toward the sky. A sky that today was the pale blue-gray of weather coming.

She smiled as inspiration filled her. Closing her eyes, she let the colors swirl behind the darkness of her lids. The rope of the swing turned from weathered tan to a shocking yellow. The seat of the swing became golden brown. It rose in her mind's eye, tossed by the wind into an azure sky.

Then she shifted her focus to the trees—their trunks slick and shiny with her black paint, bubbles of deep green like little mossy outcroppings popping up and down their mighty lengths. The leaves were in juxtaposition—the ones still attached to their branches, the stubborn ones, growing old and brown while the dead ones on the lawn became bright, alive again in golden yellows, fiery orange, and violet reds. Their veins pulsed with a blue-green blood. The grass brightened to a yellow-green, sway-ing in the breeze, then she deepened the color in her mind, adding a hint of blue. Her breath caught as the world outside her window became a fairy place where princesses and dragons roamed, a place not seen on this earth.

"Yes, the light is soft but bright." She breathed the thought aloud, imagining the slant of the sunlight and all the shadowy places. Her eyes shot open, her hand pressed flat against her beat-ing heart. Where were her paints? She *had* to get this image onto canvas before it blew away on an earthly breeze. She knew nothing this astonishing would last long in her imagination. A part of her feared it—this knowing of what she wanted and then the battle to get it down. It was always like this—elusive and frantic. But she had to try.

"Now where are my paints?" She was forever leaving things scattered about.

She turned, facing the bedroom she shared with her sister, a furrow between her brows. Mary Ann's side of the room was, of course, as neat as a pin. Hers? She grimaced. She just couldn't seem to put things back in their proper place, nor even imagine what that place might be.

She crouched down, flipped the quilt up onto the bed, and peered underneath. Ah! There was her pile of rolled-up canvas. Now, *where* were those paints? She hoped she hadn't left them somewhere, some new spot she'd found in her roamings where she had painted last. Her mother would not be pleased to find her begging for more paint.

The door banged open. Mary Ann stood at the threshold, a little breathless. "Serena, come quick! Another ship has arrived."

It took Serena a moment to comprehend that the time to paint was lost. She groaned, knowing she might not ever capture that colorful land in her imagination. A profound sense of loss touched her as she stared at the rolled-up canvas, aching for the feel of stretching it over a wood frame. But another part of her, one equally strong, wanted to help.

Serena stood, gave the canvas one last stare, and then turned to get her bonnet. "I am coming."

It was time to go. Time to leave dreams and imaginings, and do what she could to help the indentured who traveled to America on a hope and a dream.

IT WAS EVENING. The gentle rocking in the hold mocked Drake's inner turmoil. He lay curled on his side, squeezed onto the narrow confines of the cot where he spent much of his time. His arms were raised, wrapping around his head, covering his ears. His eyes were closed to the misery around him. The first few weeks of the journey proved just how stark reality had become. Seasickness was rampant. Vomit made a miserable mess of the hold, and the stench of it clung to the air, making it impossible to breathe deep. The fresh air of top deck was a distant, haunting memory. Once onto open sea, Drake had been shocked to realize that they were considered more cargo than passenger, rather like cattle than human. Basic needs and rights were now in the hands of a captain whose eyes glowed with fanatical greed. Drake knew the type— and knew the future would not be pretty for the lot of them.

Many of his fellow passengers were ill before leaving London. This combined with foul food and toilet habits added to their misery, leaving countless numbers unable to leave their cots.

Then, one by one, the dying had begun. Soon, the news came that twenty-seven people had perished. What had seemed a stunning death toll at first was now just another event in a wretchedness that left the living numb. Bodies were thrown overboard with little ceremony—those left alive hadn't the strength or spirit for formalities. The worst had been a pregnant woman unable to deliver her baby. After she and the child died, the crew didn't even bother carrying the heavy body to the deck. Instead, she was pushed through a porthole to her watery grave.

Drake curled inside himself, shunning the others in their close quarters. His fellow shipmates soon learned not to bother him unless they wanted a snarling return. He had honed the skill of verbal cuts and scornful glares long before, now it was as natural as his scowl. And as necessary.

He couldn't let them see his fear.

Each evening, as dusk approached, Drake gritted his teeth and resisted the panic. The deep of night, the pitch black, when the creaking of the old ship ruled them—that was the worst. He was afraid to sleep; for when he lost the fight, the nightmares came. It wasn't as if he'd never had a nightmare. As a boy he'd suffered them often, waking, sweat soaked, from skeletons of dead animals or fiery-eyed demons haunting him. Such nights he'd rear up, panting among his pile of blankets.

But those nightmares were nothing compared to what haunted his nights in this place.

The same and yet varied enough to never lose their terror's strength, they had the ability to wake him and leave him lying like a corpse, stilled with fear. His father, fiendishly laughed at him from the grave. Or worse, the man he'd let fall haunted him, crying from a bloody pool on the stone terrace below. Once, it was his father killing him, and another time it was his father who had pushed the man over the railing. Always the images were ghastly and Drake felt, little by little, his sanity slip away with each one.

Sleep became a dreaded thing, darkness his enemy.

When awake, Drake's mind traveled its own paths, paths his battered will could no longer resist. His memory revisited encounters he'd had with the man he'd always believed was his father. Now he doubted everything. The gossip about his mother haunted him. What he knew for certain was the hateful stares of Ivor, the contempt he'd never understood, the impotent rage underlying his actions, so incomprehensible to Drake. The questions still lingered, rearing heads that chipped away a little more and then more at Drake's identity.

Had it been Ivor's plan all along to dangle a true son's inheritance and then rip it away when the truth of Drake's lineage was revealed?

Weak, his father called him. Any show of emotion ridiculed. Any fear belittled. It hadn't taken Drake long to learn the value of becoming a shadow in any setting, as still and quiet as a piece of furniture in the castle, a ghostly form during a hunt where he secretly abhorred the killing. A silent presence at an auction of horseflesh or valuable artifacts. He was expected to watch and soak in the play of power. And he had learned his lessons well.

Then, at twelve years of age, something changed. His father began grooming him as heir. It was right and expected and everyone around them breathed a sigh of relief. Life finally took on a comforting though severe routine.

Looking back, Drake now wondered . . . Was it then that his father turned bitterness into revenge? It seemed obvious, looking back. Ivor had set upon his master plan—treat Drake as the son he'd always longed to be, waiting for the day, when he would snatch it all away.

The plotting gave his father new energy, excitement even. The subtle promises, the unequaled education, the single-minded building together of a financial empire to rival any king's—it all lead to that fateful day when father would destroy son from the grave during the reading of the will.

Who was he now? His true father, if rumor was to be believed, was an unknown uncle. The man had left him and his mother to their fate, skulking away to Bristol. How could he have done such a vile thing? Had it been Drake, he would have taken his lover and son and left England, not slink away like a dog with its tail between its legs.

All he knew was that he hated him for it.

Suddenly a sound broke through Drake's remembrance. Muffled sobbing reached him from several bunks down. The full moon lent a surreal light through the portholes, casting a ghostly gleam on the sleeping passengers. Sitting up, he searched for the sound's source. His first inclination was to turn over and ignore it, but something about the shaking of the thin shoulders, the dark tousled hair reminded him of a long forgotten memory, and he found himself going to the cot and squatting down on the rough planks of the floor.

"What is the matter, boy? Are you hurt?"

A tear-streaked face of about nine rose up from a wadded blanket that served as pillow. "Who are you?" Resentment filled the response. "I don't need nothin' from you."

Drake resisted the urge to get up and leave. Instead he sat down on the floor, settling in. "Well now, you may not, but I just woke up from a ghastly nightmare, and I was hoping you would tell me something to get my mind off it. Are you sure there is nothing you want to talk about?"

The boy sniffed and drug the sleeve of his arm across a runny, freckled nose. Propping his head on his hand he asked, "What was your nightmare about? I 'ave the same one all the time."

"Oh yes? Tell me yours and I will tell you mine."

The boy sat up, wrapping thin arms around bony upraised knees, looking half-scared and half-excited to have such a rapt audience. "The ship wrecks in a terrible storm, takes on water like the very devil and . . . people are drownin' and I . . . I'm tryin' to save my mum. She's drownin' . . . going under the waves. They always grow bigger and bigger, but somehow I'm floatin' above 'em. I–I always wake up and don't know if I've saved her or not." His voice caught but he quickly rallied, lifting that pointed chin. "Bet yours ain't worse than that 'un."

Drake smiled, feeling suddenly better than he had in weeks. "No, not worse, but equally bad. Mine involves a sea monster trying to drag me down to a cold, watery grave. Must be those beans we have been eating for our dinner. Did you have the dream tonight?"

The boy looked around and then whispered, "No, sir. I . . . I was just missin' my mother. She stayed behind with my little brothers and my sister, Ella. Pap took me and Sean with 'im to get our start." He paused and stared off into the distant moonlight. "I don't know when I will see 'er again. Or if ever I will." His voice became a whisper. "I'll see 'er again someday, don't ya think?"

"Of course you will. What is your name?"

"Danny Oliver. And yours, sir?"

"Drake—" Drake's true name hesitated on his tongue, but he held it back. Giving the boy a small smile, he finished, "Drake Winslow. Good to meet such a fine young fellow. You know, I went away to boarding school when I was about your age."

"Really sir? Can you read, then?" The lad's eyes were shining now with something far better than tears.

"Certainly. Have you had no schooling?"

Danny shook his head. "I wish I could read, though. I would most like to write. My mum says my head is full of stories. I would write them down if I could."

Drake thought back on his prized education at Eton, the private tutors he'd abhorred, something he'd taken very much for granted.

"What was boarding school like, sir?"

Everything from floggings to illicit excursions to Town flitted through Drake's mind. "Well, I attended Eton. The first two years were the worst. The older boys initiate the younger ones, you know. But then, after a time, we grew up and we became the older ones, so it evens itself out. When I was twelve my father sent down a tutor who lived with me to help me with my studies. Aside from learning to read and write, we studied Latin and Greek, arithmetic, literature, English and French and, our favorite, of course, fencing."

Danny's eyes grew wide in admiration. "Are you very good with the sword, sir?"

A bark of rusty laughter escaped Drake's throat. "Passably good, I'd say."

"I should like to go to such a school." Danny's eyes held the faraway gleam of childhood dreams. "Pap says we will have our own land in America, a place where anything is possible. Do you think that's true, Mr. Winslow?"

Drake looked into those eyes of hope and felt his spirits rise for the first time. "I hope so, Danny. I truly do hope so."

A SCREAMING WIND rose into the pitch of night, tossing the vessel into deep troughs on the turbulent Atlantic, as if they floated on naught but a pile of matchsticks. Drake clung to his pallet and tried to block out the piteous cries and prayers of his terrified shipmates. They had been on board for eleven weeks and Drake was no longer thankful he had successfully made it out of London.

He heartily wished he was in Newgate Prison instead.

At least there he would be paying for his sin. Here, he just awaited death. Would he be the next to succumb? Eleven weeks of sickness, starvation, and raspy-throated thirst made the death toll climb. Fever, dysentery, and scurvy ran rampant. Drake often rubbed a thumb against his own gums feeling how swollen they had become. His ribs poked his skin when he inhaled, a peculiar feeling, leaving him lightheaded and woozy whenever he moved suddenly. What really frightened him, though, was his lack of strength. Getting off the cot and walking to the place designated for the men to relieve themselves now brought him to a point of excruciating panting and dizziness.

A sailor came down the rickety ladder bearing a tray of biscuits. He began to pass them out, greedy hands reaching for something Drake wouldn't have conceived of eating months before. Now, his hand shook in equal anticipation. The rations, shrinking with each day, were putrid. The meat was full of worms, the water like sludge and full of worms, the biscuits infested with weevils. That men of power and wealth could treat the desolate so inhumanely was a shocking reality he now faced daily.

Life had become a horror he never dreamed existed.

As he crunched down into his biscuit Drake tried not to think about the fact that he had been one of those powerful and wealthy. Nay, not just one of them. He had been at the *top* of the powerful and wealthy. Princes from other countries acquiesced to him. And yes, he owned shares in the Virginia Company and the

East India Company, profiting from the misery of such as these sharing this dank world with him now.

He laughed bitterly, rolling a weevil around in his mouth, toying with the choice of swallowing it or spitting it out. He finished his only meal for that day in seconds and then, turning to his side, curled into a ball on the lumpy cot. His head ached from all the tortuous thoughts. He imagined drowning and the silent rest that would come with death. Maybe he was going mad. It was a grasping feeling, like he was hanging by his fingertips from the window of a high-storied building—this no longer knowing who he was, no longer knowing his place in the world. He felt like an empty skin that still had to walk and talk and eat . . . but had no soul.

You're worthless. No one wanted you and no one ever will. Just look at you. You are nothing.

Drake put his arms up over his head, covering his ears. He no longer had the strength to fight the voice that told him who he was. He could only curl up against it. Lightning flashed and thunder rolled, shaking the groaning vessel. The storm was taking a nasty turn.

Danny, several bunks away, called to Drake, fear in his tone. Drake turned toward him, desperate for a distraction. Danny had proved his salvation more than once on this hellish voyage. He saw the boy through the dim light. His thin frame draped in ragged clothes, hanging onto his cot, eyes wide. Drake's stomach turned. Watching the children endure this suffering required a different kind of bearing up than he'd yet experienced. The numbers haunted them all—only twenty-one of the original forty children were still alive.

Drake held tight to the beds on the way to Danny's cot as the ship jerked about anyone who tried to walk. Grasping the boy's thin-boned hand, Drake squeezed, panting to catch his breath so he could shout above the gale. "Is this not a grand ride, Danny?"

"My stomach hurts and I think I'm going to throw up, but there isn't anything in my stomach to come up." Danny grinned at his own joke, the skeletal smile making Drake's stomach twist harder. He remembered his breakfasts of coddled eggs and ham and toast, and how he'd thought it his due as a human, never mind as a duke. What he wouldn't give to have that golden, butter-smeared toast to give to Danny right now.

How different he could have been! Drake's chest heaved with the sorrow of it, but he rallied, became bright and encouraging, because he didn't have anything else to give Danny but hope. "Well, in that case, it's a good thing your stomach is empty. Now let us see if we can get your mind on something else. How is your reading lesson coming?"

Drake had written out the alphabet for Danny some days ago, helping the lad memorize them and the sounds they made.

"I'm up to letter *p,* sir." He put his lips together, forcing air out, making the *p* sound. He stopped suddenly as a violent cough racked his emaciated body. Drake put a comforting hand on the boy's back. When the spasm subsided, Danny blurted out, "Will you really give me a book once I 'ave it all down?"

Another dip rolled Danny into Drake, nearly knocking them both to the floor. "Of course. A gentleman always keeps his word." Drake rushed the statement, seeing the boy's eyes fill with terror as he righted them, settling the child back into his blankets.

Suddenly, a loud creaking sounded above them, which turned into a thunderous crash. Drake covered Danny's body with his own, waiting for the ceiling to cave in on them, the water to flood in. When it didn't, he looked up to see a sailor coming down the steps, water pouring into the hold.

"You there! And any other able-bodied men! We need help!"

Drake patted Danny's arm. "Hang on tight, Danny. We're men of the sea now. We can overcome this." The boy nodded, hero worship in his eyes as Drake turned from him and scrambled up to the deck, panic imbuing him with renewed strength. The ship had righted itself, but the damage to the main mast was massive. Every man available scrambled to the huge, wooden pole with its tattered sails flapping like wind-blown laundry. Drake shouldered his part of the load as they struggled to raise the beam. The wind tore at them and the weight, too much for their combined weakened state, knocked the beam out of their hands.

Again and again they tried to raise it, creaking and groaning, the men grunting and heaving, but finally, they gave up and laid it back down on the deck. They could only try again after the wind died down.

Drake's dread grew. Without the main sail it was impossible to steer the ship, which now tossed upon the gray, foaming waves like some giant child's toy. The thought of going off-track and losing time sobered them all. Rations were already slim; they couldn't afford to lose their way.

Soaked to the bone and shivering violently, Drake abandoned the attempt and, with the other defeated men, stumbled back down into the cesspool of stench that was their home.

Nothing was left to them but to wrap sodden blankets around themselves and wait to see if, come morning, they were among the living.

FOURTEEN WEEKS AND five days in the pit of a vermin-infested hold. Fourteen weeks of soul-robbing hope. Fourteen weeks of living minute by minute, and then—as a rainbow appearing—a shout was heard, echoing though the hold.

"Land!"

The word lifted them out of their desolate places.

"Land . . . ho!"

It awoke them from the depths of their despair. It was the sweetest word they had ever heard.

Drake opened his eyes, scarcely daring to believe. Land. Had they really reached it? Sitting up slowly to avoid the constant dizziness that tormented him, he listened, hoping to hear the word again—hoping he hadn't dreamed it. Others around him roused, looking like walking, crawling corpses with fanatical excitement on their faces. It was true, they'd all heard it.

Staggering to the ladder he waited in the sudden line, men and women with crazed expressions and sudden energy pulsing through their gaunt frames. They climbed the ladder with legs that shook and then stumbled across the deck to the railing. Drake recoiled from the bright dawn, their new dawn, pain shooting through his head until he thought he might collapse, but his spirit rose within him, urging the frail flesh to the rail. Behind them, a glorious sunrise pinkened the sky, washing the deck of the ship in a rosy glow. But no one spared much energy to appreciate it. They focused, as one desperate being, toward the dark line of land on the western horizon. Drake tried to hold his emotions in check as his shipmates fell apart around him—women and men wept with relief, falling to their knees in raptures of joy, grasping at the rail, unwilling to tear their gaze from the land, thanking God in loud voices that belied their weakened state. They'd reached land. They'd reached their promised land.

Drake felt a tear trickle down his hollow cheek and blinked to rid the water from his eyes so he could focus on the dark blur approaching. He found his mind repeating a lunatics' litany. *Have we really made it? Have we really found it?*

Suddenly he was kneeling. The sunlight sent bolts of pain through his eyes and into his head, but he squinted, staring at the dark coastland, willing it to arrive as nausea and excitement rolled deep in his belly. Not much sea left, his mind reminded him in a muddled fog. After so many weeks on water, land seemed a new anomaly. All he could remember now was the sea. Gray, deep, dark, unfathomable water.

He pulled himself up, clung to the rail and licked his dry, cracked lips. He watched the gentle, gray-green waves lap the ship's hull. To drink full and deep of clean, cool water. What did that feel like? Thoughts of water tormented him, memories of crystal goblets brimming with it was a dreamy image in his head, not that he ever drank much water. But now, now that he couldn't have any, he obsessed about it—its thirst-robbing authority, its crystal clarity. It even dogged his dreams. That it was all around him, and he couldn't drink it had nearly driven him insane.

Daniel McLaughlin walked up and put a hand on his shoulder. "How you be feelin' now, Drake? Fever gone yet?"

Drake squinted up from his hunched position at the only man on board he had really liked, the red-headed Scotsman, and the kind of man you would want covering your back in a fight. Drake was glad he had taken the risk and gotten to know the man.

"Not gone yet, Daniel," he croaked out, "but as soon as I can get some water, I shall recover. That is all this body needs." Drake's fever had burned hot for the last three days.

Daniel grinned, showing white teeth against an auburn beard. "Some decent food wouldna hurt much either, would it now? With land in sight, I think we just might get off this floating hell and get a little of both." He swept his hand toward the hazy coastland, his voice turning soft with conviction. "Freedom and a good life are just over those waves. Hold on for a few more hours, my friend."

Drake struggled to stand upright, and Daniel helped him back to his cot. Another day, Daniel promised—just one more day.

Pray God he survived that long.

greatness and strength. A strange sensation overtook her, making her want to reach out to him. She watched, detached from conscious movement, as her hand, small and pale, did just that. Her palm gently cupped his cheek, stroking up to his forehead, and found it burning hot. With the backs of her fingers, she smoothed his hot temple and brushed back a lock of dark hair.

Suddenly fingers as strong and tight as a manacle grasped her wrist. She reared back, about to cry out, when he mumbled incoherent words and released her. Taking a shaky breath, Serena stared. Was he delirious with fever, then? She had heard of it happening but had not seen it. She reached into her basket and brought out a cool, damp cloth, which she laid on his forehead. Taking a water bottle, she uncorked it with a soft pop and poured cool water into a tin cup. Carefully, she lifted his head. "Please, sir, drink this."

There was no response, so she tipped the cup, letting the tiniest trickle of clearness spill into his mouth. He swallowed. She smiled, caught by the moment, and tried again. He swallowed a little more, his throat moving under the growth of his beard. Again and again she fed him drop after drop of the water, exhilaration at each small success filling her, until the cup was nearly empty. Her arm ached so that she could no longer hold up his head, so she eased him back to the thin pillow and tried to make him more comfortable. Taking another damp cloth she ran it down the column of his neck and into the opening of his shirt where dark hair curled on his chest. His skin was hot and dry, heating the cloth so quickly that she had to pour a little of her precious store of drinking water onto it before starting the process again at his forehead. He grew restless, mumbling sentences that made no sense and then suddenly. "Don't call the doctor, Crudnell, he knows all. Cannot trust the man."

She had no idea what that meant, could only stare at his chiseled face and wonder if the fever would break or take him further into unconsciousness. But, more than anything she could ever remember wanting, she wanted him to open his eyes and *see her.*

After doing all she could to cool him down, she tucked the thin blanket around his shoulders and scanned the area for others. Her eyes had now adjusted to the light and she could see three more men on her side of the hold. Moving quickly to them, she assessed their condition. One was dead, the hollowness of his body showing starvation to be the likely cause. Serena pulled the blanket over his head. She would tell the captain and make sure he arranged for a decent burial. If not, the Friends would come and take the body to ensure the man had a place of rest. It wouldn't be the first time a ship's captain had shifted the responsibility. The other two were sleeping and, when awakened, were very grateful to find freshly baked bread, thinly sliced but thick with butter and water—enough water to quench weeks' worth of thirst. With healthy nourishment, Serena thought, they should be back on their feet in a few days.

Serena went over to Mary Ann's side. "How many are there?"

"Five women, one about to give birth, I think, and another with a three-year-old who is very sick. Oh, Rena—" she looked down at the floor of the hold, trying not to cry—"'tis so hard to see the little ones suffer."

Mary Ann was too softhearted to be an effective nurse, but she did her best, in between the sighs and the tears. "It is well that we are here to bring them comfort, then. Hast thou given them water?"

"Yes, and some food. They are all awake and very grateful."

"Take me to the child." Serena followed Mary Ann through the maze of cots and knelt down next to a woman and her child.

The mother lifted her head and offered a weak smile. Two of her teeth had rotted and her gums were bleeding. "Thank ye, dear ladies. I haven't been much help to little Harry here, but ye are like angels come from above. I thank God for ye."

Serena smiled at her, all the while assessing Harry. His fever was high, but he was awake and able to talk. There was no rash, which was excellent. Serena leaned toward Mary Ann. "Mostly I think they are all starved and thirsty."

Serena focused again on the mother. "Has he had loose stools, ma'am?"

"Oh my, yes. Vomiting before and the loose bowel now. Poor little chap can't keep nothin' in his stomach."

Serena reached into her basket for a jug of blackberry root tea. Dysentery was common and so she carried the tea with her on these trips. The little boy drank greedily of the sugared tea. "I will leave this here with thee," she said to the mother, "but it is for him only. Give him a cupful every two hours. I will leave plenty of good water for you and the rest of the women."

The woman smiled, nodding, and whispered her thanks as Serena moved on, Mary Ann following at her heels, to the pregnant woman.

"She says she is in her eighth month," Mary Ann whispered at Serena's back.

After assessing and talking with the woman, who was also feverish, Serena turned to Mary Ann. "She needs to be examined by Beatrice. She is such an excellent midwife. Would thee run and fetch her?"

Mary Ann nodded, relief in her eyes at the prospect of escape. "'Tis fortunate we brought Henry along as escort, else I would not be able to!"

Serena waved her away with a smile. "Yes, 'tis fortunate indeed. Let us hope our good fortune continues and Beatrice will be found at home and not out delivering a baby."

As soon as Mary Ann left, Serena's mind turned back to the man she first helped. Who was he? He seemed, somehow, so out of place here among the starving. There was an elusive beauty about him that made her imagine him in an elegant manor house, a crystal cup in his hand upraised in a toast, a troop of fawning, elegant people at his table. She had the sudden desire to paint such a scene. And him. She closed her eyes, envisioning him dressed in her watercolors. A sudden coughing made her eyes snap open. It was him. She found her feet turning, walking toward the shaft of light pooling around his bed. Mayhap he'd been caught in an earthbound spell that robbed him of his true identity.

She stared down at his face, studying it. Noting the delicate bone structure beneath the skin, she saw the deft strokes her brush would make as she painted his eyebrows, his eyelashes, his beard . . . the contrast dark and beautiful. Her gaze drifted, like a stroke of paint, down his jawline to his squared chin. A bit too thin for perfection but elegant, even delicate, with a cleft that only the careful observer would see perfectly centered under the dark growth of hair.

"How fearfully and wonderfully thou art made." She breathed the thought aloud and then turned. Had anyone heard her? She exhaled a silly smile, laughing at herself. She'd never behaved so or thought thusly in all her life. What was wrong with her?

Using great care, so as not to wake him, she sank down on the narrow edge of the cot, reaching for his forehead. It was still burning hot, making the cloth warm and dry. Exchanging the cloth for a fresh one from the basket, she pressed it against his brow, allowing her fingers to brush his temple and then back into his hair, repeating the motion until it became a gentle massage. She leaned closer still, now willing him to wake up. A fanciful thought flitted through her mind that he had been waiting for her touch to bring him back to life, that she held some power over his recovery. She smiled at herself and him, but she believed it.

His hair was black as ink, blue-black almost, and fell long and straight away from his forehead. Her fingers slid into it seemingly of their own will. Silky and inky. She imagined him with a fuller face and shaven clean. He would most certainly be handsome, but more than that, he was . . . noble. "Who art thou?"

The soft question seemed to stir something in him, for he scowled at her and answered, most imperious: "Drake Weston, fifth Duke of Northumberland, of course."

Serena gasped. "Thou art no duke!" Was he mad?

He seemed to have lost his momentary lucidity and didn't respond. Serena shook her head, staring at him for a time, then exchanged the cloth, laying a fresh one on his forehead. As she leaned back toward him she whispered, "But thee can dream of such things for a while longer, and then thee must wake up and see me."

Her husky voice sounded strange to her own ears. Her hand seemed to have a mind of its own as she touched his cheek, feeling the coarse whiskers under her thumb. It had been a long time since she had touched whiskers, and those only of her father's as he tickled her with them when she was a little girl.

The man took a long, shaking breath and seemed to sink into a deeper sleep. Her hand trailed down his neck toward his chest—

She froze. *What* was she doing? She *wanted* to touch him, and the urge had no connection to nursing. What was wrong with her? She stood, but again his hand shot out and grasped her wrist.

"Stay with me." The words croaked past dry lips.

Serena sat back down, easily conquered, reaching for the water jug for something to do. Pouring cool, clean water into the tin cup, she lifted his head to drink.

"Yes, I will stay by thy side if thou wilt drink."

He drank more this time and then dropped back onto the pillow with a sigh. She sat beside him, hands clasped in her lap to keep them from touching his face and hair, allowing herself only to watch him sleep. Her gaze fell on his lips, and she remembered the ointment in her basket. She bit her lower lip. Dare she?

A small smile formed on the man's mouth, and Serena reared back. Could he read her mind? Of course not, she chided herself. He was probably just feeling better—he'd certainly needed the water he had been able to ingest. Slowly, so as not to disturb his sleep, she leaned toward the basket on the floor and rummaged through it until her fingers wrapped around a little clay pot. It was in her lap and opened before she realized she had made her decision. She looked down at the ointment. Normally, she would have given it to the patient and allowed him to apply it himself, but this man clearly could not manage that. She dipped her finger into the pot before she could convince herself otherwise, the soothing smells of lemon and beeswax filling the space around them. Her hand stretched out toward his face, her heart pounding. What if he woke? How would she explain what she was doing?

She dabbed a bit on his lower lip and sat back to see what response he would have. Nothing. He slept on. She nodded. She was a nurse; she could do this. Leaning in again, she quickly spread the ointment across his bottom lip. He moved his head away, as if avoiding a fly, but didn't wake. Determined to finish the job, she reached for the upper lip, which wasn't quite as chapped. It was softer and curved, dark rose in color with an indention in the middle that must be sinful, it was so well shaped. Her heart pounded in her chest and her breath quickened as she spread the ointment across the top of his upper lip. She halted, realizing how close she had leaned in, how deep her breathing had become . . .

When had she closed her eyes? Heaven help her, she wanted to kiss him.

"You can, you know."

At first she didn't know if the deep voice had come from the man or some other being in the room, so deep and quiet and inside her head it was. Her eyelids shot open as she straightened. "Can what?"

"Kiss me." He smiled, but didn't open his eyes.

Serena gasped, "Thee has been awake this entire time, sir?"

One of his shoulders lifted. "I didn't think it would help my cause—" he paused pressing his lips together, as though struggling to stay conscious—"for you to realize that." Then he appeared to drop back into a deep sleep.

Serena shot to her feet, escaping her temptation and the moment, moving away from the bed to create as much distance as she could while still seeing his face. She had to get away from this man before she did . . . something . . .

As she turned, her cheeks on fire, she saw that Mary Ann was coming down the steps with the midwife. "Serena, the soul-drivers are here! They asked about these in the hold, and I did not know what to tell them. I said thee wouldst talk to them."

Soul-drivers. The name alone caused her dread. Heartless men who gathered those to be indentured off the ships and drove them house to house, farm to farm, until they were all sold. They took no regard for families, splitting children from mothers, husbands from wives. Nor did they regard humanity, scarcely feeding or caring for those who'd just survived a long, nightmarish journey.

She nodded to Mary Ann. "I will go up and speak to them." Turning to the other woman, she inclined her head. "Good day, Beatrice. Thank thee for coming. Mary Ann will take thee to the woman I am concerned about." She hurried up the stairs. If she could save these few in the hold from the horrors of soul driving, it would be some small gift. One thing she knew for certain: they would not have the man who now haunted her.

They would have to fight her for him.

Chapter Six

Frightened people crowded the deck. A tall, burly man, biceps bulging, eyes hardened, with a slashing whip hissing through the air to keep the people pinned like animals against one rail. Children wept and clung to their parents, while the adults gathered them close, their own faces mirroring confusion and fear.

Serena watched, overwhelmed by distress for the despised and desperate. They were a pitiful sight—except for one man. A tall, red-headed fellow who didn't take kindly to the treatment, as evidenced by the fact that he had engaged two of the officials in a fistfight. Serena turned away just as they caught him and pounded him to the wood of the deck. Clinging to the railing, she was able to skirt around the scene and make her way toward the ship's captain, determined to hold some rank in this world where she really didn't belong.

Captain Masters stood at the far side of the deck, his back turned away from the scene. Serena had spoken to him briefly when she and Mary Ann boarded the ship, and he'd seemed a friendly sort then. Now he appeared decidedly uncomfortable.

"Captain, might I have a word with you?"

His turned toward her as if coming out of deep thought, looking for a moment, unable to remember her.

"I am Serena Winter . . . of the Society of Friends?"

"Ah yes, what can I do for you, miss?" His gaze shifted toward the men shouting orders at the crowd. "You shouldn't be on deck at the moment. As you can see, we are, ah, trying to do business here."

"Yes, I can see that." Despite her training to be always moderate in speech, Serena couldn't keep the disdain from her voice. "There must be a better way to procure indentures for these people."

The captain straightened to his full height, looking down his nose at her. "Young miss, you haven't any knowledge in these matters." His face turned gruff and red. "What do you want?"

Oh, *why* hadn't she held her tongue. She needed this man's cooperation and riling him wasn't going to help her cause. "I wanted to assure thee and these . . . buyers that the few in the hold are not able to travel. All but one have high fevers. That one is dead."

The captain started. "Dead, you say? Gad, what a stink down there! I'll not be responsible! We've already docked, and I'm sick to death of this business."

Serena was not surprised. "Captain, perhaps we might help one another. If thou wilt assure me that those in the hold will not be moved, I will see to it that the dead man is properly buried."

A gleam lit the captain's eyes. "A little businesswoman, are thee?" At the stressed "thee," Serena gritted her teeth. The captain's eyes narrowed, and she had the distinct impression he was trying to judge her figure through the plain, gray wool of her dress and the black, hooded cape. Serena withstood the insolent scrutiny, chin raised and waiting.

"You are a pretty thing, aren't you?"

He reached out to touch her cheek, but Serena blocked his hand, leaned toward him, and took the tone of a mother admonishing a child. "Captain, I have come here to help the sick and the starving. One would think that thou wouldst know better how to take care of an investment." Her voice was quiet, peaceful even, just speaking plain truth in a way that he could do nothing but acknowledge. "Now, about those in the hold, do we have an agreement?"

The captain sighed heavily and nodded. "Sorry, miss." He pressed his lips together as he watched the soul-drivers dividing the indentured into groups. "I'm not exactly sure how I ended up in this business, you see." He looked at Serena and gave her a tight smile, then turned brisk. "I have an even better deal for you, Miss Winter. Since you are so in love with the sick ones down there, I'll sell the lot of them to you for half the price I'm getting from these soul-drivers. *You* can find them indentures. But I want them out by noon tomorrow." Almost to himself he added, "They'll probably be dead by then anyway."

With that announcement, he walked away, leaving Serena standing there, her mouth open.

What had she done? She turned, then started when she found Mary Ann and Beatrice behind her. Mary Ann rushed over. "What happened, Rena? Are they going to take the sick, too?"

"No." She looked at Mary Ann wide-eyed. "I believe I have just bought the sick in the hold . . . or promised that the Friends would."

"*What?*" Mary Ann gaped at her.

"It will be all right." Serena assured, not at all sure that was true. She turned to include Beatrice. "We will see if we can find homes for them among the Friends until they are well, then perhaps we can help them find indentures."

Beatrice, a plump, round-faced woman with a gentle face, didn't hesitate. "I will take Molly, the pregnant woman, home with me. She can stay until the babe is born and perhaps beyond that. I could use a helper, but I will have to discuss it with Foster."

Serena nodded. "Thank thee. That should help." She turned back to Mary Ann. "Father will know what to do with the rest." She hoped.

It was nearly dark when the girls got back home, rushing to the kitchen where they knew they would find their mother at this hour.

"Mother, thou wilt not believe what Serena has done!"

At her younger daughter's exclamation, Leah Winter, a pretty woman with light-brown hair and eyes, turned from the stove and looked Serena over with concern. "What has happened?"

Serena shook her head. "We are fine. It is about the indentured, is all." Serena shot Mary Ann a *don't-say-another-word* look.

Their mother nodded, smiling, soft wrinkles crinkling the skin around her eyes. "Good. Please wash up and set the table before I hear it, then. Thy sisters have been very spirited this afternoon, and I am running behind time. Father will be home any second."

The girls headed for the washbasin, knowing that doing anything else at this hour would be fruitless. Supper was always ready and waiting for their father the minute he walked in the door at six o'clock. It was a ritual not to be toyed with. And besides, they may as well tell the story to both during the meal.

With six daughters—ranging from twenty-one-year-old Serena to Lidy, who had just turned four—their father, Josiah Winter, was rather spoiled. He was waited upon, doted on, and made to feel a king from the moment he walked in till he blew